This Igloo book belongs to:

....

Published in 2010
by Igloo Books Ltd
Cottage Farm
Sywell
Northants
NN6 0BJ
www.igloo-books.com

10 9 8 7 6 5 4 3 2 1
ISBN: 978-0-85734-158-7

Printed and manufactured in China

Illustrated by: Paula Bowles, Mike Spoor, Jackie Harland,
Peter Stevenson and Gail Yerril
Stories by: Joff Brown

My Treasury of
Farmyard
Tales

igloo

♘ *Contents* ♘

The Open gate

Dog liked to patrol Daisyridge Farm and make sure that everything was just as it should be. One day, he was sniffing around the fields where the farmer grew his crops, when he found a small hole in the fence. "The farm animals could escape through this hole," he thought. "I must tell the farmer."

Dog rushed back to the farmyard, where the farmer was busy, oiling the hinges of the farm gate. Dog barked and barked to get the farmer's attention. "What is it Dog?" said the farmer. Dog wagged his tail, barked again and ran towards the field. The farmer followed him to the fence where the hole was.

However, the farmer had been in such a hurry to follow Dog, he forgot to shut the farm gate. The farm animals didn't know what to do at first. The farmer had never left the gate open before. Then, curiosity got the better of them. Even though they were very nervous, they couldn't help wondering what the world, beyond the farm, was like.

All of a sudden, Pig felt very excited. He had always wanted to see the world outside Daisyridge Farm. "There must be loads of exciting things to see," he said. With an excited squeal, he ran out of the gate. Sheep followed soon after.

The hens wanted to see the big wide world, too. Watching Pig and Sheep leave had given them courage. "Come on," they clucked, "let's go!" With that, all the hens scuttled through the gate, clucking and flapping.

The bad-tempered geese honked loudly at the hens. "We must stay here to guard the farm," they complained. They watched as Horse, Cow and her cow friends wandered out. Even Bull and the cheeky goats followed them. Before long, all the animals, apart from the geese, had left the farmyard.

When Dog and the farmer got back from fixing the hole, they were amazed to find that the farm was almost deserted. Then, the farmer spotted the open gate. "Oh no," he said. "The animals must have escaped. We've got to get them back, there are all sorts of dangers out there."

The farmer hurried out of the gate and began to run down the lane. Dog ran after him and gave a loud bark, he was worried about all his animal friends, too.

Dog and the farmer hadn't gone far when they saw Sheep. "I knew it was wrong to leave the farm," she said. "I was afraid, so I didn't go far. But the other animals have gone down the lane and some have even gone into the town."

Dog ran off down the lane, sniffing. There wasn't any sign of the farm animals, but then, Dog picked up the familiar scent of the goats and the cows. He saw them in a nearby meadow, filled with buttercups.

The goats had found some people having a picnic. The people were feeding them cakes and sandwiches and the goats were happily chomping away. "Thank goodness you've come to take the goats back," said the people to the farmer. "We've almost run out of food."

"Come along," said the farmer, "it's back to the farm for you naughty goats and cows. You won't need any food tonight," he said, "being as you've eaten most of this picnic already."

Horse had wandered quite a distance from the farm. It felt good to stretch his legs and canter across some fields. He came to a wide track, where sleek, shiny horses were running. Horse soon got talking to two of them. "We're racehorses," they said, "come and run with us." So, Horse jumped onto the track and ran as fast as he could with the other horses.

Horse had the best fun ever, racing round with his new friends. Then, after a while, he became very tired. He said goodbye and trotted happily back to Daisyridge Farm.

Meanwhile, in the busy town, the hens were feeling bewildered. The town was grey and smelly. Noisy cars and vans whizzed by and the hens were scared. "I don't like it here," said one hen. "Let's go home." So they all trouped back towards the farmhouse.

After the farmer and Dog had taken the cows and the goats back to the farm, they set out for the town. They looked all over, but could not see any of the other missing animals.

Suddenly, there was a scream from a dress shop. The sheep were wandering around, looking at everything and baaing to each other. The shop assistants were shrieking and wondering what to do. "I do like the colors on this sweater," said one sheep. "What a lovely wool coat," said another. "It's almost as nice as mine."

Dog ran in and barked, then he herded the sheep back out of the shop as quickly as he could.

In the street, the farmer spotted Bull. He was looking in the window of a shop that sold expensive china plates and teacups. "This looks interesting," mooed Bull. "I think I'll take a look inside."
"No!" shouted the farmer and he ran to catch Bull before he barged into the doorway of the china shop.

Daisyridge China

Luckily, the farmer grabbed Bull just in time. "Bulls and china shops don't go together," said the relieved farmer and led a very disappointed Bull away.

Pig was the last one to be found. He was watching the televisions in the window of an electronics store. "I must get one of these," he said, as Dog and the farmer gently steered him back towards the farm.

On the way home, they met the scared chickens. "We're never going outside again," they clucked.

At last, all the animals were safely back on the farm. Just then, the farmer's wife arrived, too. She had been shopping in the town and had heard that some very strange things had been happening. "You'll never believe it when I tell you," laughed the farmer and he went into the farmhouse to tell his wife all about the open gate.

That night, all the animals were very tired. As they settled down to sleep, everyone agreed that, even though the day had brought a great adventure, there really was no place like home!

Sheep and the Mysterious Mole

One day, on Daisyridge Farm, Sheep was on her own, in a quiet corner of the small field. She started to make up silly little songs about herself, "I am a beautiful Sheep, I'm the cleverest animal on the farm. I have the softest fleece of all the sheep and I'm full of grace and charm."

"Your singing is terrible," said a small voice. Sheep looked down to see a fat, little mole, squinting in the sunlight. "Please don't tell anyone I make up songs about myself," pleaded Sheep. "It would be so embarrassing."

"Don't worry, I know lots of secrets," said Mole, mysteriously. "When you burrow under the earth like me, you can pop out anywhere you want. I know secrets about everyone on Daisyridge Farm".

Sheep knew that she shouldn't know the animals' secrets, but she just couldn't resist. So, she asked Mole to tell her.

Mole beckoned Sheep closer. "Sometimes, Dog steals a bone from the bag of dog treats in the farmhouse. He buries the bones by the old, oak tree in the big field. He thinks nobody knows where they are, but I saw him."

"Ooh," said Sheep. "I didn't know that. It's fun to have a secret that only we know."

Mole continued to whisper to Sheep. "When one of Hen's feathers falls out, she adds it to a special nest, away from the henhouse. She lays eggs in her secret nest, so that the farmer's wife can't collect them in the morning."

"Really?" said Sheep. "Tell me more."

"When nobody is looking," continued Mole, "Horse eats turnips from the pigs' trough. The farmer tells the pigs off for being greedy, but it's not them eating all the food. Horse has never owned up to his secret munching."

Mole carried on whispering to Sheep, whose eyes got wider and wider, as she learned all the secrets of the animals on Daisyridge Farm.

Soon, it was time for Mole to go. "Goodbye," said Sheep. "Remember to keep the secret about my singing, won't you?"

"Your secret's safe with me," said Mole, with a strange, little smile.

Sheep went back to the farmyard with a big, smug grin on her face. She knew secrets about her friends and it felt good.

"How are your bones?" she asked Dog. "Still safe in the big field?"

"Have you got enough feathers for a nest yet?" she asked Hen.

"Eaten any turnips today?" she said to Horse.

Then, Sheep trotted away from the shocked animals, feeling very superior.

The next day, Sheep walked into the barn to find Dog, Horse and Hen waiting for her. They all looked rather stern. "What's the matter?" asked Sheep.

"We know you've found out all our secrets," said Dog. "You know it's very mean to spy and reveal secrets."

"It wasn't me," said Sheep, nervously. "It was that cheeky mole."
"We know," said Dog. "Mole tells everyone's secrets."

Sheep felt ashamed. "Since I know your secrets, it's only fair that I tell you mine." The other animals looked at each other. "We already know that you make up songs about yourself," they said. "Mole told us!"

Sheep couldn't help laughing. "We should catch that mole and teach him a lesson." Suddenly, there was a muffled squeak from the corner of the barn. It was Mole and he'd been spying on them. He jumped into his hole and burrowed away as fast as he could.

Dog spotted the earth rising, as Mole tunnelled along. "Quick, follow him," he said. The mound of earth moved out of the barn and into the farmyard.

The trail stopped right in front of the henhouse. Mole emerged, looking very pleased with himself because he thought he had escaped. Then, he realised the animals were chasing him, so he dived underground and carried on tunnelling.

"The trail of earth is heading straight for the big field!" cried Horse. "Don't let him get away!" Even Pig and Cow joined the chase.

Underground, Mole dug furiously. He wasn't used to having to escape and he was getting very tired. "I must be at the big field by now?" he thought. "Those silly farm animals can't have chased me this far?"

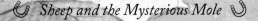

Mole began to burrow up to the surface, where he found himself right between Dog's paws. Mole was too exhausted from digging to try and escape. "Please, let me go," he said.

Sheep was very firm with Mole. "We'll let you go if you promise not to spy on anyone on Daisyridge Farm, ever again," said Sheep.

"Alright," said Mole. "I'm sorry I spied on you all. I'll leave and never return. But tell me one thing. How did you know where I was travelling underground?" "We're not telling," said Sheep. "It's a secret!"

Happy birthday, Cow!

Cow stood in the field at Daisyridge Farm. She was feeling sad and couldn't think why. "It's not raining," she thought. "The sun is shining. The grass here is very tasty. So why am I sad?"

Then Cow realised something. "I almost forgot," she said. "It's my birthday and nobody has remembered." None of the farm animals had wished Cow a happy birthday that morning. In fact, they had all been far too busy to speak to her.

Cow saw Sheep across the field. She was carrying something yellow in her mouth. "Sheep," she called. But when Sheep saw Cow, she trotted off in the opposite direction. "How strange," thought Cow.

At the duck pond, there was no sign of the ducks, or the geese. In the farmyard, the pigs rushed into the barn when they saw Cow and slammed the big barn doors behind them. Hen was the only animal that Cow could find to speak to, but she was dashing across the farmyard. Her wings were flapping and she looked very flustered. "Sorry, I can't stop," said Hen. "There's so much to do."

Cow went to see her other friends, but they didn't want to speak to her either. "Sorry," they said, when she found them in the big field. "We're extremely busy. We'll see you later." Then, they all went off across to the other side of the field. "Nobody wants to talk to me," said Cow, sadly. "I'll go and see how my favourite flowers are growing."

Cow's favourite, yellow flowers grew by the trees in the big field. However, when she went to find them, she couldn't see any. "That's odd," thought Cow, "there were lots of flowers here yesterday. I wonder what happened to them?"

Cow wandered back to the barn. Dog was lying outside the barn doors. He looked like he was keeping watch for something. When Dog saw Cow, he sat up quickly. "Go away," he barked. "There's nothing for you to see here."

Poor Cow was very hurt. Not only had everyone forgotten her birthday, now they were ignoring her and being rude. She hung her head low and wondered why everyone was being so mean.

"Dog," said Cow, sadly. Has everyone forgotten that today is a special day?"
"I don't think so," replied Dog. "Isn't it National Turnip Day? Maybe it's Halloween, or
perhaps it's Christmas instead?"

"This really is too much," thought Cow, angrily. Not only had everyone forgotten
her birthday, now they were being rude. She was about to stomp off in a huff when
she saw Pig, "Ah, there you are, Cow," called Pig. "The barn needs tidying. Can you
come and help us, please?"

"What a cheek," thought Cow, but she was tired of being on her own, so she agreed
to help. "I suppose I might as well," she said. "It's better to do something useful than
mope around all day." So, she followed Pig back to the barn.

Inside the barn, there was a big surprise for Cow. As she walked through the doors, the animals jumped up and shouted, "HAPPY BIRTHDAY, COW!."

The barn was full of her animal friends and they were throwing her a surprise birthday party.

Cow looked around in amazement. The whole barn was decorated with her all the yellow flowers she loved so much. "So that's why I couldn't find any," she laughed. "I picked them this morning," explained Sheep. "When you saw me, I was carrying them back to the barn."

"I was hurrying to help Sheep decorate the barn," said Hen. "That's why I couldn't stop to talk."
"I was guarding the barn to make sure you didn't come inside while we were getting it ready," said Dog. "I knew it was your birthday all along."

Happy Birthday, Cow!

Together, the cows and the sheep sang, 'Happy Birthday!' "The sheep have been teaching us," said the cows. "We've been practising every day in the big field." "So that is why you were too busy to stop and talk to me," laughed Cow. "It all makes sense now."

"We're sorry we've all been so busy today," said Sheep. "It's been hard work, getting everything ready for your birthday surprise, but we hope you are enjoying it." "Oh, yes," said Cow. "Thank you very much. After worrying so much that you had all forgotten, this has definitely turned out to be the best birthday ever!."

The Messiest Pig Ever

Pig wasn't happy. "I ache all over," he said to his friend, Sheep. "It feels like I've been sleeping on a pile of bricks!"

"With the state your pigsty is in," said Sheep, "you probably have!"

Pig had the messiest pigsty ever. It wasn't filled with nice, soft mud, like the other pigsties. Instead, it was filled with junk. Pig loved to snuffle around the farm and collect all sorts of rubbish.

Pig and Sheep looked at Pig's sty. Sure enough, it was filled with all kinds of trash. There was a grubby plastic doll, some green glass bottles, a pile of old newspapers and a discarded tractor tire. "You should get rid of all of this," said Sheep.

Later that day, Sheep passed the small field. She saw that someone had dumped a big heap of trash in there. When Sheep looked more closely, she realised that it was the junk from Pig's sty.

Sheep was very angry with Pig. "You can't just dump your junk here," she said. "It's making the small field look untidy. It means that everyone who walks by here has to look at your mess. What you need to do is recycle these things."

Pig didn't know what recycling meant and he didn't think it sounded very interesting. He just wanted to lie down and wallow in his lovely, junk-free sty. But Sheep was determined to find a use for the things that Pig had thrown away. So, she decided to go around the farm to speak to the other animals.

First, Sheep visited the hens. "If you could change anything about the farmyard, what would it be?" she asked.
"Our henhouse is so boring," said the hens. "We'd like a perch, or a swing, or something to play on."

Sheep dragged the tire to the henhouse. When the hens saw it, they clucked happily and sat on it. "It's all thanks to Pig," said Sheep, when the hens thanked her.

When the farmer came out of the farmhouse, he saw the hens on the old tire. "I wonder who put this here?" he said. "I'll hang it from a post, to make a perch for the hens."

Sheep went to see Horse in his stable. He was squinting in the bright sunlight. "My stable window is too big," he said. "It's draughty in the winter and in the summer, it lets in too much light and hurts my eyes."

"I think there's something we can do about that," said Sheep. She brought the green bottles to Horse's stable and stacked them in the window. "Now the window is just right," said Horse. "Thanks, Sheep."
"They're not mine," said Sheep. "They're from Pig."

Next, Sheep picked up the grubby doll and went to the farmhouse. The farmer's wife was inside. "What have you got there?" she asked and took the doll from Sheep. "I haven't seen this for years," said the farmer's wife. "I thought I had lost this doll forever. I'm going to clean her up and sew her some new clothes. She'll make a lovely present for my niece. Thank you, Sheep."

"That only leaves the old newspapers," said Sheep. "I wonder what we can do with them?"

But Sheep needn't have worried. When she went back to get the newspapers, she found the goats standing around, chewing them. "Sorry," said Big Goat, his mouth still full of newspaper. "They looked so tasty, we just couldn't help ourselves."

"Don't worry," said Sheep. "Pig won't mind you eating his old newspapers and I guess it counts as recycling."

At last, the pile of trash had gone from the small field. All of Pig's junk had been used, one way or another. As Pig trotted through the farmyard, he was surprised to find that all the animals came over and started thanking him.

"Thanks for a delicious meal, Pig," bleated the goats, when they saw him.
"We're having so much more fun in the henhouse now, thanks to you," said the hens.
"I don't have to squint in my stable anymore," said Horse. "Thanks, Pig."
"What are they all talking about?" said Pig. "I didn't do anything."

Sheep smiled and felt very pleased with herself. "I expect Pig will be sad now that all his favourite junk is gone," she thought.

Just then, Pig came trotting over looking very happy. "Thank you, Sheep," he said. "Now that my sty is clean, I've got so much more room for new things to find. In fact, I think I saw a pile of old plastic bags over by the tractor." With that, Pig ran off, ready to fill his sty with even more junk!

"Oh, dear," sighed Sheep. "It looks like he will always be the messiest Pig ever!"

Cow Loses Her Moo

It was a rainy, gloomy day on Bluebell Farm. All the animals were huddled in the barn to keep dry, but there wasn't much room. All the animals were getting restless. The sheep were practising their singing, the cows were gossiping with each other and the pigs were rolling around in their muddy sties.

The goats however, were causing trouble. As usual, they were eating anything they could find. They snatched hay from the cows' stalls and turnips from the pigs' troughs. "Someone ought to make those goats behave," said Sheep to her friend, Cow.

"I know what to do," said Cow. She cleared her throat, with a delicate little cough. Then she gave a gigantic, "MOOOO!"

The goats stopped eating and looked up. They were very surprised. "You shouldn't take other people's food," Cow said to the goats. "Why don't you sing a song with the sheep instead?"

So the goats stopped trying to eat everything and joined in with the sheep in their singing practice. "That's better," said Cow. Whenever there was trouble in the barn, Cow could always calm things down.

The next day, the animals went into the meadow. Grey clouds gathered in the sky. It looked like it was going to rain and something was wrong, too. Cow's throat was sore. Her head felt heavy and achy. "Maybe Pig will know what's wrong with me," she thought. However, when Cow tried to call to Pig, all that came out was a small, dry, croak. Pig didn't even hear it. "Oh, dear," croaked Cow, "I've lost my moo!"

The farmer soon saw that Cow wasn't well. "You must have caught a cold," he said. "We'll get you some medicine. It's about to rain, anyway, so it's about time you animals went into the dry barn."

It was very crowded in the barn again and everyone was restless. "When will this rain stop?" asked the goats. They began to practise their head-butting. Two goats would rush right at each other and smash their horns together. It made a terrible banging sound and the other animals didn't like it.

The sheep decided to practise their singing, but they couldn't agree on what song to sing. Soon, they were singing different songs at the top of their voices. It was a terrible noise. The singing and the banging made all the cows start to complain. "Awful singing," they said, "what a racket!"

When the pigs saw what was happening, they started laughing. The noise of their grunting giggles was worse than the goats' head butting, the sheep's singing and the cows' complaining put together!

"Cow," said Sheep. "You're the only one who can help, please, do something."

But Cow wasn't feeling well at all. Her head ached, she had a runny nose and worst of all, her throat felt very sore. Cow tried her best to bellow her famous moo, but she just couldn't do it. So, all the animals just carried on making noise and causing lots of very noisy trouble.

Just then, the farmer appeared. He was carrying a bottle with some medicine in. When the animals saw the farmer, they calmed down a little and the noise almost stopped. The farmer gave the medicine to Cow. "That will make your cold better," he said and gave her a pat.

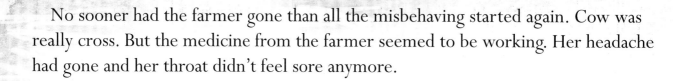

No sooner had the farmer gone than all the misbehaving started again. Cow was really cross. But the medicine from the farmer seemed to be working. Her headache had gone and her throat didn't feel sore anymore.

The terrible din continued and it was getting worse and worse. It was making Cow's head hurt again and she was getting very, very, angry.

Without even thinking, Cow lifted her head, opened her mouth and let out the longest, loudest, "MOOOOOOOO!" that any of the animals had ever heard.

Suddenly, all the animals stopped. There was total silence. No one was in any doubt that Cow had definitely got her moo back. "That's better she said. "I think what we all need is a nice, soothing story."

The animals liked this idea. So, they all settled down and Cow told them a bedtime story. Soon, even the noisiest animals were feeling sleepy. They yawned and stretched. "Time for bed," said Cow. This time, everyone did as they were told. At last, the barn was quiet. "I'm glad I got my moo back," said Cow and she settled down to sleep.

Goose's Flying Start

It was another lovely day on Bluebell Farm and Goose was being his normal, bossy, self. "Out of my way," he honked, pushing the chickens to one side. "I can't stand you useless birds. You can't even fly. What's the point in a bird that can't fly?"

Hen was a bit timid at times, but she'd had enough of Goose's bullying. "If you're so good at flying," she said, "why have I never seen you fly? All the other geese fly around the farm, but you never do. Let's see you fly today," she said.

Goose suddenly looked very nervous. "I'm too busy to fly today," he said, then he waddled away, as if he was in a hurry to go somewhere.

Cow was listening and thought it was all very strange. She followed Goose to the green field and found that he wasn't busy at all. In fact, he was sitting on his own, staring moodily at the duck pond.

When Goose saw Cow, he frowned at her. "Go away," he hissed. "I'm far too busy to fly". Cow started to question Goose. "WHAT is it that you are so busy doing?" she asked. "You don't herd the sheep like Dog. You don't give milk, like me. You don't even lay eggs, like Hen."

To Cow's surprise, Goose started to cry. He made a loud, honking noise, like an old car horn

"There, there," said Cow. "What is it, dear?" She put her nose down and let Goose cry on it.

"I'm scared of flying," said Goose. "I'm not very good at it. What if I can't keep up with the others? What if I get lost? What if I crash into the ground and everybody laughs at me?" Goose cried even louder than before. "I don't want the other geese to know, or they'll make fun of me."

"It wasn't very nice of you to be so rude to Hen, if you can't fly yourself," said Cow, sternly. Goose just honked louder than ever.

"I'll help you practice flying, if you like," said Cow. "But you have to promise to be nice to all the animals on the farm."

"Oh, all right," said Goose, bad-temperedly. "But I don't see how a cow can help me to fly?"

"I'll show you," said Cow and she gave a long, "moooo." Suddenly, all kinds of wild birds flew down to the pond. "These are my friends," said Cow. She asked the wild birds if they would help Goose to fly and they said they would be happy to.

So, every afternoon, Goose, Cow and her bird friends met in the furthest corner of the green field, where nobody would see them. The wild ducks showed Goose how to take off with huge, powerful strokes of his wings. A falcon showed Goose how to glide on the wind for many miles. The swallows showed Goose how to loop and twist in the air. Even the swans helped, by showing Goose how to land gracefully in the stream.

At first, Goose really was terrible at flying. He bashed into trees and he bounced off the ground. When he first tried to land in the stream, he went right under and came up spitting out water.

Goose was very surprised to find that none of the wild birds made fun of him, even when he made a mess of all his lessons. They all tried as hard as they could to help. Slowly, Goose got better at flying. After a few weeks, he was able to take off, flap through the air and land as gracefully as any swan.

As Goose got better at flying, something else changed as well. He remembered not to be so rude to the other animals. He stopped laughing at them and calling them names. He even tried helping out on the farm, picking up any rubbish he saw and helping to keep the farmyard tidy. In fact, he was so happy at learning to fly properly, he simply forgot to be nasty.

One day, Hen reminded Goose about his promise. "You said you'd show us your flying skills, remember?"
Goose was very nervous, but he tried not to show it. "Alright then," he said, "I will."

Cow wandered over with some of the other animals. "You can do it," she whispered, so that only Goose could hear.

Goose plucked up all his courage. He ran as fast as he could and flapped his wings until he thought they would fall off. Then, Goose looked down and found that he was gliding over the farmyard. He flew round the farm in a big circle and saw that all the other animals had gathered to watch him.

When Goose landed, Hen thought that he was going to laugh at her, because she couldn't fly. But instead, Goose said, "Hen, I'm sorry I was so rude to you. Flying isn't easy." Hen was amazed and clucked with pleasure.

"I never thought I'd see Goose be so nice," said Pig. "It's amazing. Did you have anything to do with it?" said Pig to Cow. But Cow just winked and said nothing.

All the farm animals thought that Goose was like a changed bird. Goose was so happy, he forgot to bully anyone ever again. Only Cow knew why Goose had become so good at flying and that she had given him a flying start.

The Big Storm

Sheep was feeling very pleased with herself. She had just counted all the other sheep in her field. "I must be the cleverest animal on the farm," she thought to herself. "If only all the other animals were as clever as me. It's hard to be the only smart one around here."

Sheep saw Dog, as she passed by his kennel. He was staring up into the sky. "I counted all the sheep," she said. "Knowing how many sheep there are will help you to herd us."

Dog didn't seem very impressed. "I saw some grey clouds in the sky," he said, "I think there's going to be a storm."
"Oh, Dog," said Sheep. "If you stopped looking at the sky and started taking better care of us sheep, the farm would be a better place."

Sheep skipped past Horse, who was chewing some hay in his stable. "I heard a rumble of thunder," said Horse. "Sheep, do you think there will be a storm?"
Sheep ignored his question. "I counted all the sheep," she said. "There were twelve of them. I bet you couldn't do that?"

Sheep went through the farmyard and saw Hen scratching in the dust for seeds. "Hen," she said. "I counted all the sheep on the farm."
"Never mind all that," said Hen. "There's a storm coming. I'm sure I felt raindrops on my feathers a minute ago."

"Oh, Hen," said Sheep. "You're always getting flustered over nothing. If there was a storm coming, I'm sure I would have noticed."

Sheep decided to go for a long walk across the field, just to make sure she hadn't missed counting any of the other sheep. But the field was empty. As Sheep trotted along, she felt something on her woolly back. It was a raindrop. "Hmm," said Sheep. "How strange."

Soon, it began to rain. At first, there were only a few drops, pitter-pattering down. But then the rain began to fall in huge sheets.

The ground grew muddy and Sheep found that she was slipping and sliding all over the field. She saw a flash of lighting and heard a big rumble of thunder.
"Oh no," said Sheep. "Dog, Horse and Hen were right. Now I'm stuck out in the field, in the middle of a storm."

Sheep looked around, trying to find somewhere that would keep her dry. She saw a big tree in the middle of the field. "I must get under that tree," she thought. But, as she raced towards it, a big bolt of lightning struck the tree. Sheep didn't dare go anywhere near it.

Sheep was cold and scared, too. But most of all, she felt sad about the way she had treated her friends. "They all told me a storm was coming," thought Sheep. "But I was too proud to listen. I bet they're all safe and snug in the barn, laughing at me."

But the animals weren't in the barn at all. They were out looking for Sheep. Horse and Dog were in the rainy farmyard. Dog sniffed the ground. "I think she went this way," he said, and they ran off towards the field, followed by Horse. The rain came down so heavily, they could hardly see.

Sheep was very cold and bedraggled. "Help," she called in a small voice. She was in the middle of a big puddle of mud. Horse clopped through the mud, easily. He helped Sheep back to where Dog was waiting. All three animals hurried back to the safety of the barn as fast as they could.

Sheep was very glad to be back at the farm. "Thank goodness," said Hen. "Come inside, where it is warm and dry. "We were so worried about you."
"I'm sorry I was so rude to you," said Sheep.

"Don't be silly," said Hen. "I didn't even notice. I'll stay here with you tonight instead of going to the henhouse." So, Hen roosted next to Sheep. Her feathers were very warm and it was like snuggling up to a feather mattress.

Outside, the storm raged. Raindrops drummed loudly on the roof of the barn and one of the doors kept squeaking and creaking. It was all just a bit too scary and Sheep found it difficult to get to sleep.

"Are you alright, Sheep?" asked Hen. Sheep didn't want Hen to know how scared she was. She was about to say, "I'm fine," when she thought how kind Hen had been. "I can't get to sleep," Sheep admitted. "It's too scary and noisy."

Hen thought for a minute. "I know something that might help," she said. "Do you remember how you counted all the other sheep in the field?"
"Yes," said Sheep, looking puzzled.

"Well," said Hen, "why don't you try counting them all again, but in your head?" People say counting sheep makes you fall asleep."

So, Sheep thought of all the other sheep in the field. She imagined them jumping over a gate, one by one. Every time one jumped over, she counted it. "One sheep, two sheep, three sheep, four sheep… " It was very restful. Before she got to five sheep however, Sheep was fast asleep!

When she woke up in the morning, she peeked out of the barn door. The storm had finished and the sun was shining. The rain had washed over the farm and everything looked bright and clean. Sheep skipped outside, happily and all that day she made sure that she listened to her friends.

"Where are you, Cow and Pig?"

Pig and Cow had been bored at Bluebell Farm all day long. It had been so hot, no one wanted to move. The sheep chewed grass lazily in the meadow and Dog slept by his kennel in the sun. Now that the cool air of evening had come however, Pig and Cow tried hard to think of something exciting to do.

"I know, let's go exploring," said Pig.
"We know everywhere on the farm already," Cow reminded him.
"Then let's go outside the farm," said Pig. "The farmer hasn't mended that fence that fell down in the big field. Let's go and explore the woods beyond it. I'm sure we can find lots of great things to do. We can find flowers and look for lizards and play hide and seek."

Cow thought about it. She knew she wasn't meant to leave the farm.
"Alright then. But let's not go too far," she said. "It's getting late."
The sun was already low in the sky by the time Pig and Cow set out across the big field. They found the broken fence and squeezed themselves through.

The woods looked wonderful. The trees formed a great green roof over their heads as they explored. Little patches of golden sunlight danced over them. They even followed the stream that ran from the farm. "As long as we keep next to the stream," said Pig, "we'll find our way back easily."

Pig and Cow went deeper into the wood, then they came upon a big clearing, which was filled with bluebells, like a bright, blue carpet. Cow and Pig spent ages playing in there.

After a while, they noticed that the woods were getting dark, as the sun went down.
"I'm hungry," said Pig. "Let's go back to the farm."
But Pig and Cow couldn't remember the way to the little stream.

They wandered through the wood, but there wasn't any sign of the stream anywhere. Soon, they were back among the bluebells, but now it was getting cold and dark. "It must be this way," said Cow, choosing a different path. But this one led them to a part of the woods they were sure they hadn't seen before.

Back at the farm, the farmer was checking over all the animals, as they went to sleep. He saw that Pig and Cow were missing. "I wonder where they could be?" he thought.

Meanwhile, Pig and Cow were truly lost. The forest looked different at night. It was very quiet and the trees seemed to lean over them. Strange little breezes floated around, making them shiver. Whichever path they took, Pig and Cow always seemed to end up back at the clearing filled with bluebells.

"What's that white shape, peering over the trees?" said Cow. "That's just the moon," said Pig. He jumped as he heard a low hooting sound. "What was that?"

"I think it was an owl," said Cow. Suddenly, a big, feathered shape swooped over to them, without a sound. "Can I help yooou?" hooted the owl.

"We're lost," said Pig. "Do you know the way back to Bluebell Farm?"
The owl stared at him with its round eyes. "Noooo, sorry," it said and flew away.

The moon disappeared behind a cloud and the woods became even darker.
"I'm sure I heard something," said Cow. "This time, it wasn't an owl."
Pig cocked his pink ears and listened. Cow was right. It sounded like a voice. It was calling their names.

Cow and Pig ran and hid by a gigantic oak tree. "What if there are ghosts in this forest?" whispered Pig. "What if this forest is haunted?"
"Don't be silly," said Cow. "There's no such thing as ghosts." But she huddled close to Pig anyway!

A dark shape came into sight, calling in a deep voice.
"Where are you, Cow?" said the voice. "Where are you, Pig?"
It was the farmer. He had come out to the woods to look for them.
"Hooray," squealed Pig. "We're saved." The scared animals stepped out from their hiding place.

"There you are," said the farmer. "What silly animals you are, coming out this late at night. I'd expect it of you, Pig. But I'm surprised you went along with him, Cow." The animals felt rather ashamed. They hung their heads all the way home. But at least the woods felt much less scary with the farmer there.

When Cow and Pig got back to the barn, they told the other animals all about their adventure. "Cow was really frightened. But I wasn't scared at all," said Pig. Then he heard a long, low sound. He jumped into the air. He turned to see Cow mooing! Cow started to laugh and all the other animals joined in.

"Okay," said Pig. He couldn't help laughing, too. "Maybe I was a bit scared. I won't be going into the woods at night again, I promise!"

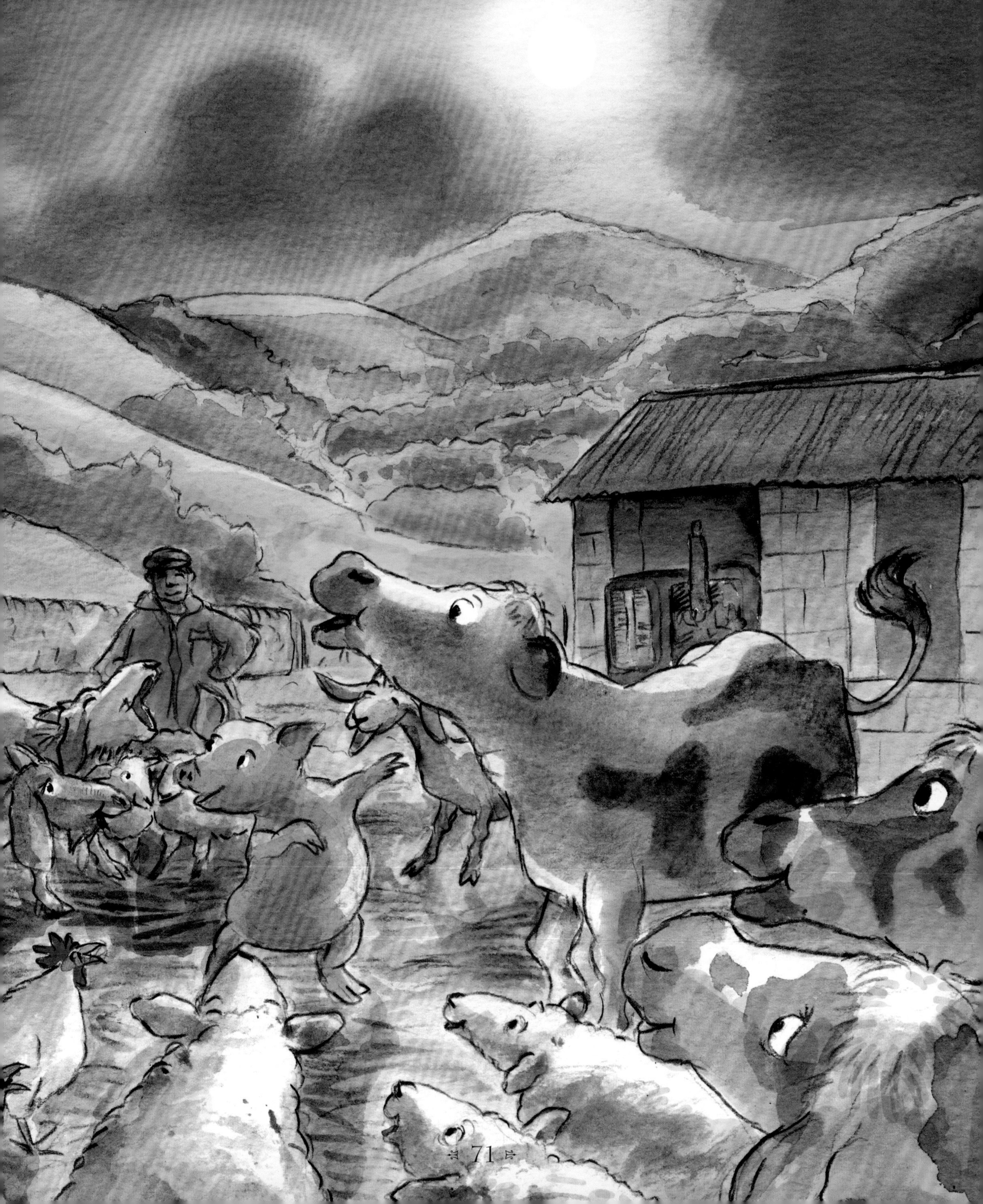

The Squirrel Burglars

It was early in the morning on Sunnycroft Farm and the farmer's wife was in the kitchen. "It's going to be a busy day on the farm," she said to herself, "but if I get time, I think I'll do some baking."

The farmer's wife went to the larder and found some walnuts, hazelnuts and almonds. "I'll use these nuts to make a delicious nut cake," she said. The farmer's wife put the nuts in a bowl and left it on the kitchen windowsill while she went off to do her chores.

Later on, Dog was walking around the farmhouse, sniffing, when he heard some strange noises. There was a scratching, a scampering and lots of giggling. Dog looked up at the window. There, on the windowsill, were three squirrels looking at the bowl of nuts. "Let's steal these nuts," said one of the squirrels. "We can take them home and have a nutty feast."

"Oh, no," thought Dog. "We've got squirrel burglars!" He barked loudly. "Hey, you squirrels, leave those nuts alone. They belong to the farmer's wife."

The startled squirrels scampered away onto the thatched roof of the farmhouse. "We're not scared of you, Doggy!" shouted one, cheeky squirrel. "We'll get those nuts soon," said another, shaking its tiny paw.

Dog tried to jump up and catch those naughty squirrels. However, try as he might, he couldn't quite reach the thatched roof. He barked and barked until the farmer came along to see what the fuss was about. "Why are you barking at the roof, Dog?" asked the farmer. But when Dog looked up, the squirrels had gone. The farmer walked off, shaking his head.

All morning, Dog watched out for the squirrel burglars. Then, he saw them in the thatched roof, chattering and laughing at him. Dog knew they were working out a plan to steal the tasty nuts, but each time he barked at them, they hid.

The other farm animals wondered why their friend was barking so much. When Dog told them why, they didn't believe him. "Whoever heard of squirrel burglars?" laughed Sheep. "You must be dreaming," said Cow.

Dog was upset that no one believed him. It was his job to guard the farm and he was determined those mischievous squirrels would not steal the nuts.

Later on, Dog came back from the small field and saw that the squirrels had climbed down the thatched roof. They were just about to sneak into the kitchen. Dog sprang up to the window, barking and yelping.

The chattering squirrels scampered away, but suddenly, Dog found that he couldn't move. He was stuck in the half-open window!

Just then, the farmer's wife came into the kitchen. "Dog, what on earth are you doing?" she said. "You really are behaving very strangely." She pulled Dog through the window and closed it behind her. "I must remember to make that nut cake tomorrow," said the farmer's wife, looking at the bowl of nuts.

That night, when all the animals on the farm were asleep, Dog settled down in his kennel. Suddenly, he heard the familiar sound of scratching and scampering. The squirrel burglars were back!

Someone had left the farmhouse door open and the squirrel thieves were in the kitchen. They were looking up at the bowl of nuts. Dog was just about to bark when he had a thought. "If I bark and the squirrels run off, nobody will believe me. They'll think I'm making things up again."

Dog looked around the kitchen. Near the bowl of nuts was a big, round, cake cover made of wire. Suddenly, Dog had a idea. He crouched low and crept quietly behind the squirrels.

The squirrels were so busy looking at the nuts, they didn't notice Dog tip the cake cover with his nose. It fell down over two of the squirrels and they were trapped.

The third squirrel dashed out of the kitchen, into the hallway. Dog scrambled after it, barking loudly. The squirrel tore up the stairs and ran right into the farmer's bedroom.

The farmer's wife got such a shock, she screamed! The farmer jumped out of bed and threw a sheet over the squirrel. Now it was trapped, too.

Dog rushed back downstairs, barking and wagging his tail. The farmer and his wife followed Dog into the kitchen, where they turned on the light and saw the trapped squirrels. "So, that's why you were barking, Dog," they said.

"Let's take these little thieves to a new home," said the farmer. He took the squirrels to a forest far away, where he let them out. The squirrels never came back to Sunnycroft Farm ever again.

"Well done, Dog," said the farmer's wife, "you're a very clever boy. As a reward, you can have this delicious bone."

The farmer's wife gave Dog a big bone to chew. Dog took it to his kennel, wagging his tail, happily, all the way. After all, he didn't have to worry about those squirrel burglars any more!

Wake up, Dog!!

It was early morning on Sunnycroft Farm. Cockerel sat on top of the henhouse. He usually crowed at dawn, but today, he had a bit of a sore throat. Luckily, the farmer's wife was already up and was busy milking Cow. In the farmyard, the sheep waited for Dog to herd them into the small field, but he didn't come.

Dog was still asleep, lying in his kennel, with his paws in the air, snoring. "Wake up, Dog!" oinked Pig. "The sheep are waiting to go out into the field." Dog yawned and stretched. Then he looked at the sun, rising high into the sky. "Oh, no," he barked. "I'm late again."

The sheep were running around the farmyard and the farmer was cross.

"Where were you, Dog?" he shouted. "You should be up at dawn, ready to work. If you can't get up on time, I'll have to think about getting another sheepdog." Poor Dog put his tail between his legs and hung his head.

The next morning, the farmer's wife found rabbits chewing at her cabbages. "Dog is meant to chase them away," she said. "Where is he?"

Dog was asleep in his kennel again. "Sheep tried dangling a tasty bone in front of his nose. "Wake up, Dog!" cried Sheep. But Dog didn't even twitch. The rabbits nibbled their way happily through all the farmer's wife's cabbages and she was very cross with Dog.

The following day, a couple of stray dogs came and growled at the goats in their pen. The goats were very frightened and Dog was still asleep. "Wake up, Dog!" neighed Horse, "the goats need your help." But Dog didn't move.

So, Horse took a bucket and filled it with water from the river. He returned to Dog's kennel and tilted the bucket with his nose. The water splashed all over Dog's head. But Dog just shook himself, yawned and carried on sleeping. The goats bleated in fear, until Horse trotted over and drove the stray dogs away himself.

The farmer and his wife saw Dog sleeping in his kennel. "I don't know what's the matter with that dog," said the farmer. "If he doesn't wake up on time over the next two days, I'm going to find another sheepdog."

Hen heard what the farmer had said and rushed off to tell the other animals. "We MUST find a way to get Dog up in the morning," she clucked.

Meanwhile, Dog was thinking of a way to wake up early himself. "I want to be a good sheepdog and help the farmer," he said to Pig. Suddenly, Dog had an idea. "I'll stay up all night," he said. "That way, I'll be awake when the sun comes up." "I don't think that will work," said Pig. "Everybody needs to sleep." But Dog didn't listen.

That night, when the sun went down, Dog lay in his kennel, staring at the moon and stars. "All I have to do is keep my eyes open," he said to himself. "Then I'll see the sun come up." However, before he had even finished speaking, Dog was fast asleep!

The next morning, because he had stayed up so late, Dog was awake later than ever. "If Dog doesn't wake up tomorrow on time," said Hen, "the farmer will buy a new sheepdog. I don't want a nasty new pooch chasing me and barking all the time."

"We've tried everything," mooed Cow. "Nothing will wake Dog. Maybe now that Cockerel's throat is better, he will crow again at dawn."

Pig snorted and then grunted with delight. "I've just had one of my brainwaves," he said. The other animals gathered around to listen to Pig's plan.

That night, when Dog had gone to sleep, the other animals tiptoed out to his kennel. They picked it up and began to move it, very quietly and carefully. Then, they crept back to their own, warm beds and left Dog snoring.

Early next morning, Dog was still fast asleep. He was dreaming about herding sheep and chewing big, meaty bones. Suddenly, right by his ear, there was a very loud, "COCK-A-DOODLE-DOO!"

Dog jumped into the air with fright and ran straight out of his kennel. "What's going on?" he said, still half asleep. When Dog looked around, he was very surprised to see that someone had moved his kennel right next to the henhouse. Cockerel was sitting on top, crowing as if he had never had a sore throat. The sun was just coming up and, at last, Dog was awake in time to herd the sheep.

From that day on, Dog never had to worry about getting up on time. All the animals realised that Cockerel's sort throat was the reason Dog kept sleeping in. Now, with his kennel next to the henhouse, Dog was always woken up by Cockerel's morning call.

After that, Dog herded the sheep on time, every morning. The farmer was very proud of him. "He's like a new sheepdog," said the farmer to his wife. "I wonder why he suddenly started waking up on time?"

The farm animals smiled at each other. Thanks to Pig's brainwave, Dog had his own personal alarm clock. Never again would they have to say, "Wake up, Dog!"

Pig Saves the Day

Pig loved the farmer's red tractor. He thought its giant wheels and shiny, red body were the best thing he'd ever seen. When nobody was looking, he would sniff around it and watch how it worked.

Soon, Pig knew more about the tractor than any other animal on the farm. "I could drive that tractor," he thought to himself. "The farmer turns the wheel to steer it. It can't be too difficult to turn a wheel."

Not long after, the farmer and his wife were away for the day and nobody was near the tractor shed. Pig went in and looked at the tractor. "It's so shiny," he said to himself. "It can't hurt just to climb into the cabin."

So, Pig jumped up onto the tractor and sat behind the wheel. "I wonder what this red button does?" he thought and he pushed the button with his trotter.

Suddenly, the tractor's engine rumbled and roared into life and the cabin started shaking. Pig had switched the tractor on by mistake. "All the animals will hear," thought Pig. "I'd better switch it off."

In a panic, Pig pushed all the buttons he could find. Suddenly, the tractor started to roll forward, out of the tractor shed. It rolled into the farmyard, scaring the hens. Pig tried pushing more buttons and pulling the levers, but the tractor just went faster.

Pig tried to steer, but his trotters couldn't hold the steering wheel. Afraid that the animals might see him, Pig ducked down in the cabin and hid.

The runaway tractor whizzed all over the farm. It rattled over the old bridge to the small field. It zoomed around the field and back to the farmyard. It trundled straight into the barn and roared right out the other side.

The hens flapped and squawked. Sheep and Cow had to dive out of the way. "Someone has to stop the tractor!" cried Hen.

After zooming round and round the field, finally, Pig pressed the right button and the tractor chugged to a halt. All the animals rushed over and found Pig climbing out of the cab.

Pig didn't want his friends to think he was foolish, so he told a lie. "I was taking a walk, out in the field and saw the tractor moving. I jumped in and stopped it. It's a good job I was around, or who knows what might have happened," he said.

All the animals were very impressed. They thought about what Pig had said. The tractor might have knocked down fences, or flattened the wheat, or even run the animals over. "Well done, Pig, you saved the day," they all said.

After that, everyone on the farm treated Pig like a hero. He had to tell his made-up story about how he stopped the tractor, again and again. The animals were so impressed, they brought him lots of tasty treats, like cabbages, turnips and carrots.

However, Pig knew that telling lies was wrong. One day, he decided to tell the truth. "The tractor didn't just go out of control on its own," he said to the animals. "It was my fault. I wanted to drive the tractor and was messing around with the buttons. I'm not a hero at all. I lied to you."

The farm animals looked sad and disappointed. They walked off, without saying a word and left Pig, all alone, in the middle of the farmyard.

A few days later, the farmer was driving the tractor when he hit a big lump in the farmyard. The tractor skidded and fell on its side. The farmer tried to open the door and get out, but the door was stuck.

Sheep saw what had happened. She ran to where Pig was sitting, all on his own, in a dark corner of the barn. "Pig, we need your help!" she cried. "You know how the tractor works."

"No," said Pig, glumly. "Whatever it is, I'll just mess it up."

Sheep explained that the farmer was in trouble and immediately, Pig rushed to help. He had spent so long looking at the tractor, he knew exactly what to do. "The door lock must have jammed when the tractor toppled over," he said. "I think we need to give the door a whack," said Pig. "That should make it unlock."

Pig ran to fetch Bull. "We need you to charge at the tractor, as hard as you can," he said. So, Bull backed up and charged right at the tractor, hitting it with his horns. The door sprang open and the farmer was freed.

This time, everyone knew that Pig really had solved the problem.

"If you hadn't told the truth about driving the tractor," said Sheep, "we would never have called on you to help."

The farmer was very relieved to escape from the tractor and that night, he gave all the animals some extra treats to eat. Pig was munching some sweet, juicy turnips when the other animals came to say good night. "Well done, Pig," they said. "This time, you really did save the day."

Pig smiled and snuggled down in the straw. "It feels good to be a real hero," he said and fell fast asleep.

How Horse Got His Tail Back

The farmer's wife was in the stable, grooming Horse. His coat was shining, his mane was bright and his tail was thick and glossy. "You stand a good chance of winning a prize in the farm show, next week," she said. Horse was very pleased. He liked the idea of winning a prize.

Horse loved to scratch himself and sometimes, his tail would lose some long hairs on the fences and gates around the farm. But for weeks, Horse had been very careful. He hadn't stood near any fences, or rubbed against any gates. His tail was perfect and he wanted to keep it that way.

The next day, Horse was trotting towards the old bridge when he heard a loud honking coming from the henhouse. "That sounds like the geese," said Horse, trotting over to the henhouse.

"Help us, Horse," honked Goose, from inside. "We went to sleep in here, while the hens were in the farmyard, but the door closed and we're trapped."

"Hold on, I'll get you out," said Horse. He pulled at the door gently with his teeth until it opened. All the geese rushed out, flapping and honking. "Thanks, Horse," they said, as they waddled off to the duck pond.

Horse turned to go, but he didn't notice that the end of his tail had got stuck in the henhouse door. He walked off, leaving tail hairs trailing from the hinges.

The next day, Horse was munching some oats when Pig ran up. "Can you help us, Horse?" said Pig. "The farmer promised us the turnips on the cart, but he's gone to the market. Can you tip the cart up, so we can get the turnips?"

Horse pushed the cart with his nose until all the turnips tumbled out. The pigs munched on them happily, in between grunts of thanks. Horse didn't notice that some of his shiny tail hairs had got caught in one of the cart's wheels.

The next morning, Horse was walking by the field when he heard Cow, mooing, loudly. "Something's wrong with Cow," thought Horse and he cantered over to the fence. "What's the matter?" he asked.

"It's Sheep," said Cow. "She's hurt her foot. Please, fetch the farmer."

Horse galloped back to the farmhouse and whinnied until the farmer came out. The farmer knew something was wrong and he followed Horse to the field.

Soon, the farmer had treated Sheep's sore foot. But, Horse didn't notice that some of his tail hair had caught on the field's fence.

On the way back to the farm, Horse stopped to look at his reflection in the duck pond. He looked at his shiny coat and his glossy mane. Then, Horse noticed that his tail was thin and wispy. There was hardly any hair left in it.

When The farmer's wife saw Horse's tail, she shook her head, sadly. "Oh, dear," she said. "I thought you were going to be good this week."

Horse whinnied with annoyance. It wasn't fair that the farmer's wife thought it was his fault. "I'll never win a prize at the farm show now," he thought.

The geese, pigs and cows heard about Horse's missing tail and decided to help. They checked the henhouse, the turnip cart and the fence in the field. Soon, the animals had found lots of Horse's hair. They left it in a pile, outside Horse's stable.

That evening, the farmer's wife came to prepare Horse for the farm show. She saw the pile of hair by the stable. "How strange," she said. "I wonder how this got here?" Then the farmer's wife had an idea. "I've got some colored bits of string," she said. "I'll use it to braid Horse's hair back into his tail. It will be as good as new."

When the farmer's wife had finished, Horse looked very smart. He had ribbons in his mane and his tail was braided with bright colours.

At the farm show, the judges looked at Horse and wrote notes on their clipboards. At last, the results were announced. "Winner of the Best Groomed Animal prize is, Horse, from Sunnycroft Farm," said the head judge.

The judge pinned a big, red and blue rosette onto Horse's mane. He was the proudest horse in the show.

Everyone at Sunnycroft Farm cheered when Horse returned.
"Thank you for helping me," said Horse, when he found out what the geese, pigs and cows had done. Horse had helped them when they most needed it and all the animals were glad to return the favour.

Horse wore his prize rosette proudly, every day. But ,the farmer's wife never did find out how Horse got his tail back!

The Farmyard Games

Horse and Dog were standing in the farmyard, arguing again. Everyone on Holly Farm was bored of listening to them. "I can run the fastest," said Dog. "That's rubbish," said Horse. "I'm much faster than you."

"Why don't you have a race to find out who's the fastest?" asked Sheep. "Then you can stop talking about it all the time."
Horse and Dog agreed. "What a good idea," they said.

"Of course, if it was jumping, then I would win," boasted Sheep. "Everyone knows that, as well as being the cleverest animal on the farm, I'm also the best jumper."
"You?" said Pig. "I don't think so. Nobody can jump further than me."

Soon, all the animals in the farmyard were arguing about who was best at sports. Cow gave her loudest, "MOOO!" Everyone stopped talking and looked at her.
"I think," said Cow, "that it's time to have more than just a race. Let's have the first, official Farmyard Games!"
All the animals were very excited. "This is going to be fun," they said.

"We'll hold the games in one week's time, in the field," said Cow. "There will be running and jumping and all kinds of contests. You'd all better get practicing."

That week, all the animals began to exercise, all except Pig, who was far too lazy. While Dog and Horse spent their time running across the fields, Pig sat in his sty. Sheep saw him dozing and laughed. "You'll never beat me at jumping, Pig," said Sheep, "you're too lazy."

Pig thought hard. "Maybe Sheep's right," he said to himself. "Maybe I should exercise." So, Pig tried stopped eating so much and wherever he went, he jumped up and down. "What's got into that pig?" wondered the farmer. "He's always jumping around the farmyard."

One day, after finishing his exercises, Pig searched through the junk in his sty and found some old Christmas decorations that the farmer's wife had thrown out. They were pretty and still glittered brightly. "These will make perfect medals for the winners," he said and took them to show Cow.

Finally, the day of the farmyard games arrived. All the animals lined up in the field for the first, short race. Cow started the race with a loud, "MOOOO." The animals dashed off and Dog managed to sprint ahead of Horse to win.

"And now, the long distance race," said Cow. This was a much longer race, all the way to the long field. At first, Dog raced ahead, but by the time he had got halfway, his legs were getting tired. He slowed down and Horse saw his chance. He galloped past Dog to win the race.

The Farmyard Games continued all day, with lots of different events. The ducks and the geese watched as they flew over the fences and fields. Sheep did the high jump and then watched Pig doing the long jump. Horse and Goat raced each other and Dog had a wonderful time pole-vaulting.

"I wonder what all the animals are doing in the long field?" said the farmer's wife, looking out of the farmhouse window. "They look like they're having fun."

By the end of the day, the only animal who wasn't happy was Hen. She was coming last in most of the events. "I'm not good at sports," she thought. "I'm not the fastest, or the strongest and I can hardly fly, but I suppose taking part is what matters."

Soon, Cow announced the winners. "Fastest animal, long distance is, Horse. Fastest animal, short distance is, Dog. Highest jumper is, Sheep. Longest jumper is, Pig."

When she had read out all the winners, each one was given a shining decoration to wear as a medal. "Oh, and there's one more prize," said Cow, smiling. "The Farmyard Games Special Prize for effort goes to, Hen."

At first, Hen couldn't believe that she had won something. "Me, a prize?" she clucked, happily. She was given a shiny, gold decoration. She wore it proudly around her neck and flapped around the field, so everyone could see.

As the sun went down over the long field, the animals tramped back to the farmyard. They were exhausted, but very happy. It had been a wonderful day, full of fun and laughter

That night, the farm was quieter than it had ever been, as all the animals fell into a contented sleep. "I'm worn out," yawned Horse, as he returned to his stable. "I wonder which animal is the most exhausted of all?"

The most tired animal was the only one who hadn't taken part in any event and that was Cow. Organizing the Farmyard Games had taken all of her energy. But, as her sleepy eyes closed, she was still planning. "The Farmyard Games will be even bigger and better next year," she thought and she drifted off into a deep sleep.

The Big Parade

The farmer's wife was very excited. She was making a float for the big parade that was going to go through the nearby town. The float was on a trailer and it was going to be pulled by the farmer's red tractor. "The float will show everyone all the animals on Holly Farm," said the farmer's wife.

First, she covered the trailer in green paper, so it looked like grass. Then she spent many days making life-size models of all of the animals on the farm. She made models of Dog, Hen, Cow, Pig, Sheep and Horse.
"This horse doesn't look anything like me," said Horse, when he saw his model.
"They're not finished yet, silly," said Sheep.

The next day, the animals all watched as the farmer's wife brought in rolls of coloured paper and started to cover the model animals. One by one, the model animals began to look just like the real ones.

Hen looked at her model suspiciously. "I hope they don't replace me with this wire and paper version," she clucked. At least it can't lay eggs, like me."
Dog growled at his model. "I'm the sheepdog around here," he said, "not you!"

Sheep laughed at them. "Don't be silly," she said. "These are just for the float. When the parade is done, these models will be taken apart."

Finally, the float was finished. Everyone agreed that it was a spectacular sight. The animals all looked very real. "It's so exciting!" said Pig. "I can't wait to see the float roll through the town tomorrow."

"You know we're not allowed to go into town," said Cow to Pig. "I guess we'll never get to see the parade."

"Oh," said Pig, feeling quite upset. "I really wanted to see it."

That night, the farmer's wife left the float in the middle of the farmyard. However when all the animals were asleep, a huge wind blew up. It howled around the barn and ripped some of the tiles from the farmhouse roof.

Worst of all, the wind blew over all the animal models on the back of the float. They all fell into the muddy yard. The wind kept blowing. It blew so hard that it tore all the models apart and they were ruined.

The next morning, Pig was the first to see the mess. The animals gathered around the ruined float. "The farmer's wife is going to be very upset," said Cow. "If only there was something we could do."

Pig thought harder than he had ever done before. "Wait," he said. "I have just had an amazing idea. I think there's a way we can save the float and we can all get to see the parade, too." Pig snuffled at the back of the trailer until the ramp came down.
He trotted up it and started pulling off the remains of the models. "We need to clear the space," he said.

When the trailer was empty, Pig told the other animals to get up onto the trailer.
"What are we doing?" asked Hen.
"Don't you see?" said Pig. "We can be our own models." There was just enough room for all the animals to squeeze onto the trailer.

As soon as they were all on the float, the animals saw the farmer coming into the farmyard. "Remember," said Pig. "Stay very still, so that the farmer and his wife can see what we're trying to do."

The farmer tutted at the mess the wind had caused. Then he saw the animals all standing very still on the float. He called to his wife. "I think the animals want to be part of the parade," he said. He took his flat cap off and scratched his head in amazement. "I've never seen anything like it."

The farmer's wife came out and saw all her precious models, blown to pieces by the wind. Then she saw all the real animals standing very still at the back of the trailer. She gave them all a big, sunny smile. "Thank you all," she said. "You've saved the float. But you'll have to be very careful if you want to stay on there."

The farmer started the engine and the tractor pulled and pulled until the trailer began to move. There was a big jolt and for a moment, the animals thought that they were about to fall off. But then, the tractor began to tow the trailer slowly out of the farm. They were on their way.

The red tractor pulled the trailer all the way down the farm lane. The animals mooed and barked and oinked, as the wheels went over bumps in the road. "Hold on tight!" cried Pig, "it's going to be a bumpy ride." All the animals laughed, they were having lots of fun.

The parade through the town was a wonderful occasion. There was a marching band and bright balloons, as well as all kinds of floats from lots of other places.

When the farmer drove the tractor up the high street, past all the shops, the crowd clapped and cheered. They had never seen a float with real animals on it before. The float from Holly Farm was the best one in the parade.

The farmer and his wife felt very proud of the animals, as they rode in the big parade. But it was Pig who felt the proudest of all.

Hen and the Sly Fox

One day, Little Hen was picking bluebells on the edge of the wood. "These will look nice in the henhouse," she thought, "the other hens will love them."

But in the dark wood, someone was watching. He was red and furry, with a long, bushy tail and glinting, black eyes. Sly Fox stepped out. "Hello," said Little Hen. "Who are you?"

"My name is Reginald," said the fox. "What a beautiful bouquet of flowers you have. I must say, they match the colour of your eyes." Little Hen blushed. "Thank you, you're very kind," she said.

The sly fox wanted to know all about the farm and all the other hens that lived in the henhouse. In fact, the fox was very, very interested.

When Little Hen went back to the farm, she told Sheep all about the fox. Sheep was not at all happy. "That fox is up to no good, Little Hen," she said. "He wants to get into the henhouse so he can gobble you all up!" "Reginald is so nice," said Little Hen. "I'm sure you're wrong."

But the next time Little Hen went out picking flowers, she was more wary. When she saw the fox, she didn't go right up to him. Instead, she hid in the undergrowth.

Little Hen heard Sly Fox talking to himself. "I'm so hungry," he was saying. "I haven't had a proper meal in days. But soon, that feather-brained Little Hen will lead me right to her henhouse. Then I can get inside and eat all the hens!"

When the fox had gone, Little Hen rushed back to the farm, as quickly as she could. She found Sheep and told her what she had heard.
"The fox was right, I am feather-brained," said Little Hen, sadly. "If I had invited him round to the henhouse, who knows what might have happened? I'm going to set a trap for our foxy friend."

Little Hen went and found Dog, who was dozing in his kennel. She told him her plan. "It's rather dangerous," said Dog. "But of course I'll help you."

The next day, Little Hen set off for the woods again. Sure enough, she saw the fox. But this time, he wasn't so friendly. When he saw her, he put his paw on her and pinned her to the ground. "I'm feeling hungry," he said, licking his lips. "I think I'll eat you for my lunch."

"Don't eat me, Mr Fox," said Little Hen. "If you let me go, I'll leave the henhouse door open tonight. Then you can get in and eat as many hens as you want!" "Hmm," said the fox. "Alright, but remember to leave the door open." He took his paw off Little Hen and she fluttered away as fast as she could.

That night, the sneaky fox crept into the farmyard. He looked around carefully, but he saw no sign of any dogs, so he crept up to the henhouse.

Sure enough, the door was open. The fox slipped inside and peered around. All the hen roosts were empty. He could only see Little Hen, sitting on a big pile of straw. "Where are the other hens?" said the fox. "It's time for my dinner." "They had to go away, tonight," said Little Hen. She tried not to sound scared.

The fox was angry. "Then I'm going to eat YOU!" he growled and got ready to pounce. Suddenly, a tail poked out of the straw that Little Hen was sitting on. Then the straw began to move. It rose up and fell away. Little Hen was actually sitting on Dog's head. He had been hiding, waiting to catch the fox.

Dog gave his best, scary snarl and the fox backed away in fright. Suddenly, the smart, sly fox was lost for words. He gave Little Hen a long, hungry look and began to move backwards towards the henhouse door.

Little Hen was very relieved that the nasty fox hadn't eaten her up. Her feathers were all of a quiver. She watched, as Dog crouched low and the fox moved slowly away. Suddenly, Little Hen flapped and Dog jumped at the fox, snarling, barking and growling. The terrified fox turned and quickly scrambled out of the henhouse, as fast as he could.

There was a terrible commotion, as Dog chased the fox round and round the farmyard. The fox yipped in fear and Dog barked as loudly as he could. They even woke the farmer up who came to see what was going on.

The farmer stood in the farmhouse doorway, watching Dog chase the fox faster and faster. "Good dog," he said. "I'll put some wire up tomorrow, so the fox can't get into the henhouse."

After that, Dog chased the fox right out of the farmyard. The hens were safe in the henhouse and the sly fox was too scared to come near Daisyridge Farm ever again.

The Shiny New Tractor

Horse loved to work hard at Appledale Farm. He pulled the plough in the field until all the ground was churned up, ready for seeds to be sown in it. He carried the cart full of milk and vegetables to sell in town. He was so strong, he could even pull down trees, if the farmer tied ropes to them. As a reward for all his hard work, the farmer gave Horse all the hay, carrots and sugar cubes he could eat. And that was a lot, because Horse was always hungry!

One day, Horse was munching some hay in his stable when he saw the farmer drive into the farm in a big, shiny, red vehicle.

"It's not a car," said the hens, "its wheels are too big."

"It's not a truck," grunted the pigs. "Because it's got a big trailer behind it."

"It's a tractor," said Sheep, who was very clever. "It's for helping the farmer around the farm. It can pull the plough, take food into town and do all sorts of things."

Horse looked at the tractor and frowned. "But that's what I do," he said. The tractor got its own shed, right next to the stables where Horse slept. That night, Horse gazed at the shiny new tractor.

The next day, it was time to plough the small field. Horse cantered over to the field, ready to get tied to the plough. But the farmer was already driving the shiny red tractor over the field. The plough was joined to the back of the tractor. "Sorry, Horse," the farmer called out. "There's nothing for you to do here."

Once a week, the farmer's wife liked to ride Horse around the farm, to check that all the fences were straight and the fields weren't overgrown. Horse waited for the farmer's wife to come and saddle him up, but she never appeared. Then Horse looked over the fields and saw that the farmer's wife was driving the shiny red tractor all over the farm. She looked very happy.

Pig saw that Horse looked sad. He asked him what was wrong. "It's not fair," said Horse to Pig. "Why should the tractor have all the fun?"

"Don't be sad," said Pig. "You can still do some things a tractor can't do."

"Like what?" asked Horse.

"Erm… you can eat," said Pig. "And be my friend. A tractor can't do that."

But Horse still felt sad. What was he going to do on the farm now?

That night, rain pattered down on the barn and the farmhouse. In the morning, everyone in the farm woke up to find that the river had flooded. The whole of the small field was turned to thick, gooey mud. Some of the trees had fallen over and were blocking the stream.

"I must go and move those trees," said the farmer. Horse was very excited at the thought of helping the farmer out. But the farmer walked right past the stables and went to the shiny red tractor. He drove the tractor over the bridge, into the small field.

But the mud was very thick indeed and soon it splattered all over the tractor's windshield. The farmer couldn't see where he was going. He drove too near the river, where the mud was thickest. When he tried to drive the tractor away, he found that it was stuck. No matter how hard he tried, the tractor wouldn't move at all. And it was slowly sinking into the muddy river bank and down towards the river.

When the farmyard animals saw what was happening, they squealed and clucked and mooed and made such a loud noise that the farmer's wife came out to see what the fuss was about. "How can we get the tractor out of the mud?" she said.

Horse knew what to do. He clopped over the bridge to the field. His big, wide hooves hardly sank in the mud at all. And he was careful not to go too near the river bank. The farmer's wife came with him. The farmer threw her some ropes and she attached them to the tractor. Then the farmer's wife tied the ropes to Horse's harness. "Pull, Horse!" said the farmer and the farmer's wife. "Pull as hard as you can!"

Horse strained at the ropes, trying to pull the tractor out of the mud. It was very heavy, but he kept pulling and pulling as hard as he could.

"Don't give up, Horse!" shouted the farmer. "It's nearly moving."
With a mighty effort, Horse tugged the tractor with all of his might. With a huge sucking sound, the tractor came free of the mud and Horse pulled it back onto the solid earth. "Well done, Horse!" said the farmer. "It looks like there are some things only a horse like you can do around here." Horse neighed and tossed his head. He was very tired, but happy.

Later that day, when the farmer had cleaned up the tractor, he drove it back into the farmyard. Its trailer was filled with all kinds of tasty oats, hay and vegetables. "I guess the farmer's taking the food into town on the tractor now," said Horse. "Maybe he doesn't need me after all."

But the farmer stopped the tractor in the middle of the farmyard and led Horse to the trailer. "This is all for you, Horse," said the farmer. "It's a reward for saving the tractor. I bought the tractor because I was worried you were working too hard. I didn't want to wear you out. But there's still plenty of work for you AND the tractor to do."

Horse whinnied with joy and tucked straight into the feast. The other animals laughed to see him chomp down the food so fast, but Horse didn't care. He was enjoying the best meal of his life.

Horse and Duckling

One morning, on Appledale Farm, Horse was strolling by the duck pond. Suddenly, he heard a peculiar, cheeping sound coming from the reeds on the edge of the pond. When Horse looked, he found a strange-looking grey duckling. "You're an odd little fellow," said Horse. "Where are your parents?"

The little duckling didn't answer, he just started to cry, "Aw, don't do that," said Horse. He bent his head down to get a better look. The little duckling waddled up to Horse's big muzzle. It made its funny squawky cheep and jumped up onto his nose and ran all the way up his head and sat between Horse's ears.

Horse let the duckling ride on his head, all the way back to the stable, where they settled down for the night. Horse made a little nest out of straw and the little duckling snuggled into it. "Tomorrow, we'll find your mother and father," Horse promised the sleepy duckling. "But for now, I will watch over you and make sure you are safe. The little duck gave a contented, "quack," then went to sleep.

The next day, Horse took the duckling to the ducks on the pond. But they didn't know anything about the little bird. "What an ugly creature, he's not one of us," they quacked and swam away.

Horse visited the hens to see if they knew anything about the duckling. But the hens were too busy pecking at corn to pay them much attention. Only Horse's friend, Hen, was interested. "I've never seen a duckling like that before," she clucked. "Most ducklings are yellow-colored, but he's grey. It's very peculiar."

Later that day, Horse had to pull the cart into town. "You stay here," he said, leaving the duckling with Hen, "she will look after you."

But, when the farmer's wife came to throw the corn out for the hens, Hen rushed over to feed and forgot all about the poor, little duckling, who wandered off on his own around the farm.

When Horse got back from town, he couldn't find the duckling anywhere. He searched and searched, but there was no sign of him. "I'm sorry, Horse," said Hen. "It was here a minute ago, I'm sure."

Eventually, Horse found the duckling on the pond, in the middle of a circle of geese. They were laughing at him and calling him names. The duckling didn't really understand what was going on, but he didn't look very happy.

Horse was very angry. He stomped over to the geese and when he was behind them, he neighed as loud as he could.

The geese were all frightened and fell silent. Horse drummed his hooves hard on the ground, scaring the geese so much that swam off across the duck pond. "Don't listen to those cruel geese, duckling," said Horse. "They're just a bunch of mean bullies. We'll find your parents soon, don't worry."

Every day, Horse looked out for the ducklings parents. Every day, the little duckling got bigger. His neck got longer, his bill stretched out, and his wide, grey feet got even bigger. Most of the other animals thought he was getting even uglier, but not Horse. "It doesn't matter what you look like," he told the duckling. "Look at me, I'm big and my feet are wide, but I'm proud of that. It helps me be strong and work hard for the farmer." The duckling quacked, happily.

One day, while Horse munched some grass by the duck pond, he saw two lovely, white birds swim up the stream and into the pond. They had long necks and orange and black beaks. They looked very graceful and beautiful. "Excuse me," said one of them. "Have you seen a little grey bird around here?"

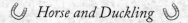

Before Horse could answer, the little grey duckling came waddling up. "That is our little cygnet," said the swan. "We were so terribly worried about him. Thank you for taking such good care of him."

Six more little cygnets came swimming up. The little cygnet greeted them with happy cheeps and quacks, then they all began to play together.

Now Horse realised why his little friend had seemed so strange. "You're not a duck at all," he said. "You're a swan!"

The little duckling looked at Horse and said goodbye.
"We'll come back soon," said the mother swan. "When we return, our baby will have grown into a beautiful, adult swan."

Horse went back to the farmyard. He felt very sad that his little friend had gone. But Dog comforted him. "Just think," he said, "all the animals on the farm will want to hear the story of Horse and the duckling. That made Horse feel a lot better.

Bull's Big Day

One morning, on Appledale Farm, Little Pig found his friend, Hen, looking sad. "What's the matter?" asked Little Pig.

"I really want some juicy berries," said Hen, "but they only grow in Bull's field. I'm scared to go there in case Bull chases me."

"He won't chase you," said Little Pig. "Everyone knows that Bull is harmless. Don't worry, I'll get the berries for you."

So, Little Pig dug a hole under part of the fence by Bull's field. He squeezed his little body under it and went to pick the berries. But Bull saw him. He snorted and roared and charged towards Little Pig who ran away, terrified that he would be tossed over the fence.

Suddenly, Bull stopped. "Oh, what's the use," he snorted. "I wouldn't hurt a fly and everybody knows it. Nobody's scared of me anymore. The goats all bully me, the geese laugh at me and I even get pecked by the hens.

Little Pig felt sorry for Bull. "I thought you were very scary," he said. "Look how fast I ran from you." But Bull didn't hear Little Pig, he just wandered back to his pen, and stood there, sighing and looking upset.

Little Pig took the berries back to Hen. She was very happy that Appledale Farm had such a timid Bull. But Little Pig wasn't so sure.

The next day, the Farmer led Bull out to the farmyard. Little Pig watched and saw that what Bull had told him was true. The goats sniggered and tried to knock him over by head butting him. The hens laughed when he wasn't looking. Worst of all were the geese. They called Bull all sorts of horrible names.

"Poor Bull," said Dog to Little Pig and Horse. "It's not fair that he gets bullied all the time."

"I know," said Little Pig. "I'm going to come up with one of my special plans. When we're finished, nobody will ever bully Bull again. Will you two help me?"

"Of course we will," said Dog and Horse.

Little Pig went to see Bull when he was back in his pen. "It wasn't always like this," said Bull. "Everyone used to think I was big and strong and fierce. But I have feelings, just like everybody else. Once I banged my nose on the gate. It really hurt and I bellowed. Goose called me a big baby and it really upset me. After that, all the geese called me names and nobody was scared of me any more." Bull was very sad. A couple of big tears rolled down his big, brown face.

Little Pig decided to cheer Bull up. "I've got a plan," he said and whispered in Bull's ear, so that the chickens and the geese couldn't hear. Bull listened to Little Pig, then he blinked away the tears. He thought for a second. Then his face brightened and he began to smile.

The next day, when Bull was allowed into the farmyard, Little Pig came up to him. "Hey, Bull," he called out, so everyone in the farmyard could hear him. "I think you're just a stupid waste of farmyard space. You're more like an overgrown mouse than a bull!"

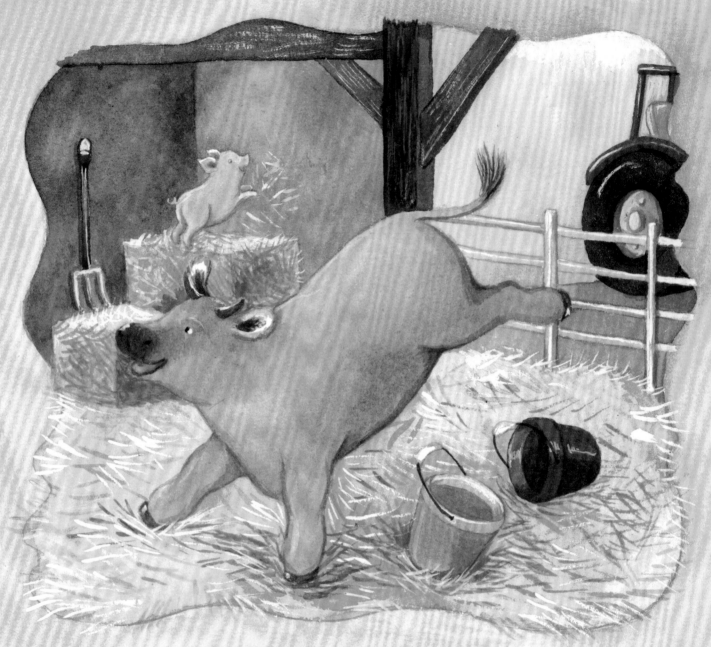

Bull turned to look at Little Pig. "I've had enough!" he roared. "I'm going to teach you a lesson you'll never forget, Little Pig."

Little Pig ran into the empty barn and Bull followed him, making sure that he roared and stamped around a lot on the way. Inside the barn, Bull and Little Pig stopped running. "It's going well so far," said Little Pig. "Now we have to pretend that you're chasing me around the barn and tossing me in the air with your horns." So, the two animals made as much noise as they could in the barn. They jumped on all the hay bales. They bashed into the wooden walls. And they shook the metal gates, with loud crashing sounds.

All the animals were listening outside. "Is Bull really chasing Little Pig?" they wondered. "That's not like him." They thought this was very strange. Then, Dog ran up. "Stand aside," he said. "I'm going to rescue my friend, Little Pig, from that terrible bull."

Dog slipped into the barn, where he joined in with Bull and Little Pig making lots of noise. Then Little Pig and Dog ran out of the barn. "We were lucky to escape," they told the other animals. "Whatever you do, don't make Bull angry."

Horse trotted up. "I'm going in there," he said. "Surely Bull can't beat a big, powerful horse like me?"

"Don't go in!" cried Little Pig and Dog, just like they had rehearsed. "It's too dangerous."

Just as they had planned, Horse went into the barn and he and Bull had lots of fun making even louder crashing and banging sounds. Horse ran out of the barn, pretending to be scared. "Help!" he whinnied. "Bull is the scariest animal on the farm."

Now it was time to see if Little Pig's plan had worked. Bull came out of the barn. He was out of breath from all the noise he'd been making and he looked fierce and dangerous.

Bull looked at Goose. "Do you have anything to say to me?" he snorted, loudly.
Goose looked at Bull, then at Pig, Dog and Horse who were lying in a heap trying
to look defeated. "Sorry I was so mean to you," said Goose, swallowing nervously.
Bull felt very proud of himself and soon all the animals who had bullied him said they
were very sorry.

From that day on, nobody bullied Bull again. "It's all thanks to you," said Bull to
Little Pig. "It's good to be respected again."
"It's better than good," said Little Pig. "It's incredi-BULL!"

Who Let the Goats Out?

Early one morning, Appledale Farm echoed with some very strange noises. There was a rattling and clattering, plus lots of clip-clopping followed by munching and crunching. Someone had let the goats out of their pen when no one was looking. It happened just before dawn, when most of the animals were still half asleep.

The greedy goats trip-trapped all over the farm, looking for tasty things to gobble up. They ate Horse's oats and scoffed all the food in the pigs' trough. They even licked up the hens' corn from the ground.

When the animals got up to have their breakfast, they found that there wasn't any food left to eat. Nobody could work out who had opened the goats' gate, or why. The farmer wasn't happy at all. It took him ages to round up the fat-tummied goats and herd them back into their pen.

When Pig heard what had happened, he decided to solve the mystery of who let the goats out. "Leave this to me," he said. "I, Pig, the great detective, will discover who did this. I will, of course need to interview everyone, just like a real detective."

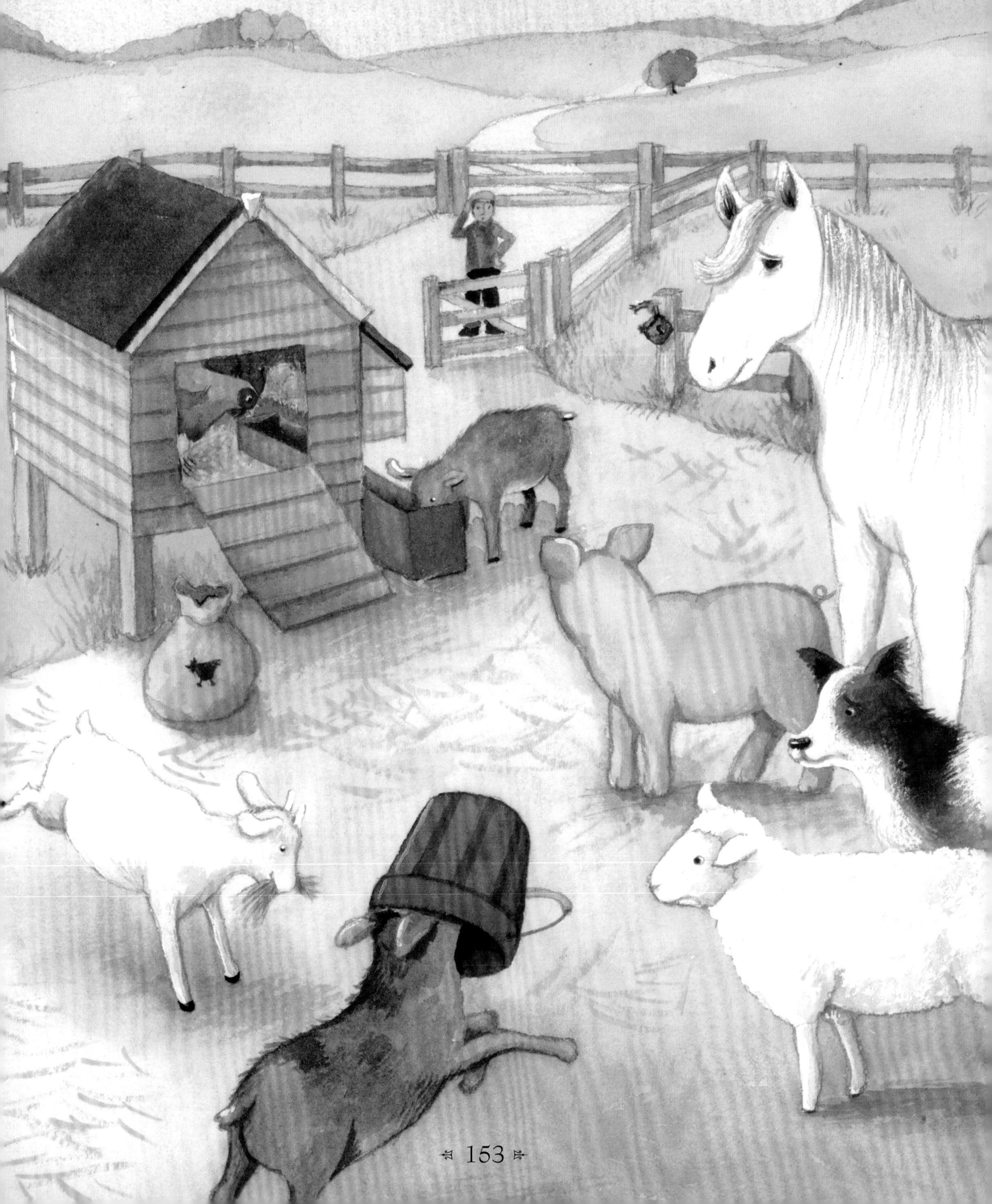

The first person he spoke to was Sheep. "So, Sheep, if that is your real name," he said. "Were you near the scene of the crime, this morning? Did you let the goats out of their pen?"

"Of course I didn't, silly," said Sheep. "You saw me this morning when you were trying to find mushrooms."

"Interesting," said Pig, who was trying to act like a real detective. "That could be an important clue."

Next, Pig went to see Big Goat and his friends who were safely back in their pen. "We didn't notice anything," Big Goat said. "We woke up early and found the gate open. Then we went out and ate everyone's lovely food. It was delicious!"

Pig noticed that the lock on the goat pen was old and shaky. It would have been easy to knock open.

"Where were you this morning?" Pig asked Hen, next.
"I was in the farmyard, near the goat pen," said Hen. "Don't you remember? I said hello to you. You were sniffing for mushrooms."
"Aha!" said Pig. "That's right. So you were at the scene of the crime?"
Hen just looked at pig and sighed.

Next, Pig went to see Dog. "I saw you wandering around the farm early this morning," said Pig. "Did you open the goat pen?"
"I didn't," said Dog. "I was getting ready to help the farmer herd the sheep to the fields."
"Of course," said Pig. "The farmer and his wife are sure to have valuable clues to help me solve this mystery."

So, Pig sneaked quietly up to the farmhouse. He saw that the kitchen door was open. The farmer and his wife were inside, talking to each other. Pig listened carefully. "We really must find out how those goats are getting out," said the farmer. "It took me ages to get them back into their pen. They even chewed my trouser leg!" The farmer's wife chuckled.

Suddenly, the farmer saw Pig poking his head into the kitchen. "Pigs are not allowed in the farmhouse, out you go," said the farmer, firmly.

Pig ran squealing back into the farmyard. He really was terribly excited. "I've learned another important clue," he said to himself. "I think I have all the evidence I need." Pig called all the animals into the barn. "I have called you all here today, to reveal the mystery," he said. "I have discovered who let the goats out."

The animals looked at each other and smiled. To be polite, they sat quietly and waited for Pig, the great detective, to solve the crime.

"Here is what happened," said Pig, grandly. "Dog planned it all. Horse used his strength to force open the gate to the pen. Hen clucked loudly to wake the goats up. Then, Sheep shooed them all out into the farmyard. It was a big plan to make sure Horse's dry oats got eaten, so he would be given juicy carrots instead."

The animals stayed very quiet for a while, then they burst into hilarious laughter. "Pig, you are silly," they said. "That's impossible."
"I told you I wasn't there," giggled Sheep.
"I can't even cluck very loudly," chuckled Hen.
"The gate wasn't forced open, Pig," Horse reminded him.
"And I'm not clever enough to plan anything," said Dog.

"Ah," said Pig. "That's a bit of a problem then." He looked puzzled. "Perhaps I haven't solved the mystery yet."

"Pig," said Sheep, "I think you've forgotten somebody."

"I doubt it," said Pig. "I've asked everyone on the farm."

"Pig, you were up first this morning," said Hen, "I saw you."

"You were looking for tasty mushrooms all around the farm," said Dog.

"And YOU sniffed around the goat's pen," added Horse.

Everyone knew that when Pig was snuffling for mushrooms, he went everywhere and forgot everything.

Pig thought very hard for a while. "Yes, I remember now. I was looking for mushrooms and I thought I could smell one near the goat's pen, so I rooted and rooted and I rattled the pen gate until I found a big, delicious mushroom underneath it. As soon as I had eaten it, I went back to sleep. All the rattling must have opened the lock. That means it was me who accidentally let the goats out!"

Poor Pig felt very foolish, but his friends said it didn't matter. "You might not be the best detective," they said, "but at least we know who let the goats out!"